Good Dog Carl
and the
Baby Elephant

Carl, I'll bet you and Madeleine would enjoy this.
I'll take you to the Zoo on Saturday.

Good Dog Carl
and the
Baby Elephant

Alexandra Day

LAUGHING ELEPHANT · MMXVI

LAUGHING ELEPHANT · 3645 Interlake Ave. North, Seattle, Washington, 98103

ISBN/EAN: 9781514900222

Copyright © 2016, Alexandra Day
First printing · Printed in China · All Rights Reserved.

LAUGHINGELEPHANT.com · GOODDOGCARL.com

Here's where you go in.
I'll pick you up about 3 o'clock.
Have a good time!

Uh Oh. I think the elephant is stuck.

Push, Carl!

Hello, Carl!

Hey Carl, I just heard a radio announcement that there's a baby elephant missing from the Zoo.

Thank you, Carl.
We were worried about him.